P9-DMC-549

The Terrible Trash Trail

Eco-Pig Stops Pollution

By Lisa S. French
Illustrations by Barry Gott

visit us at www.abdopublishing.com

For Alex, Yvonne and Victoria—LSF

Published by Magic Wagon, a division of the ABDO Group, 8000 West 78th Street, Edina, Minnesota 55439.

Printed in the United States.

Manufactured with paper containing at least 10% post-consumer waste

Text by Lisa S. French
Illustrations by Barry Gott
Edited by Stephanie Hedlund and Rochelle Baltzer
Interior layout and design by Nicole Brecke
Cover design by Nicole Brecke

Library of Congress Cataloging-in-Publication Data
French, Lisa S.
The terrible trash trail : Eco-Pig stops pollution / by Lisa French ; illustrated by Barry Gott.
p. cm. -- (Eco-Pig)
Summary: In rhyming text, Eco-Pig wakes up from a nap only to find his beautiful town of To-Be totally trashed.
ISBN 978-1-60270-663-7
[1. Stories in rhyme. 2. Pigs–Fiction. 3. Pollution--Fiction. 4. Green movement--Fiction.] I. Gott, Barry, ill. II. Title.
PZ8.8.F9085Te 2009
[E]--dc22

2008055332

It was another grand day
in the town of To-Be.
Eco-Pig napped
in the green apple tree.

Yes, all was in order,
so clean and so neat,
from the hairs on each head,
to each home on each street.

The roses were rosy
and the sky was deep blue.
The songbirds were singing
and the hedgehogs were too!

E.P. was snoring,
dreaming his favorite dreams
of wide-open fields
and clear, bubbling streams.

But something was happening,
something not right!
And when E.P. awoke,
he got quite a fright!

E.P. could not deny it,
he had to confess.
From river to roadside,
To-Be was suddenly a mess!

There was a trail with flat tires,

a rusty paint can,

and plastic bags by the dozen.

The town was not spick-and-span!

E.P. said, "I must get to the bottom
of this foul-smelling pile!"
"But how?" cried Louise,
"It goes on for a mile!"

They followed the trash trail
through the town of To-Be.
They went past the park and through
the forest to the edge of the sea.

While E.P. got busy
giving garbage the sack,
Louise turned to see
they were still under attack!

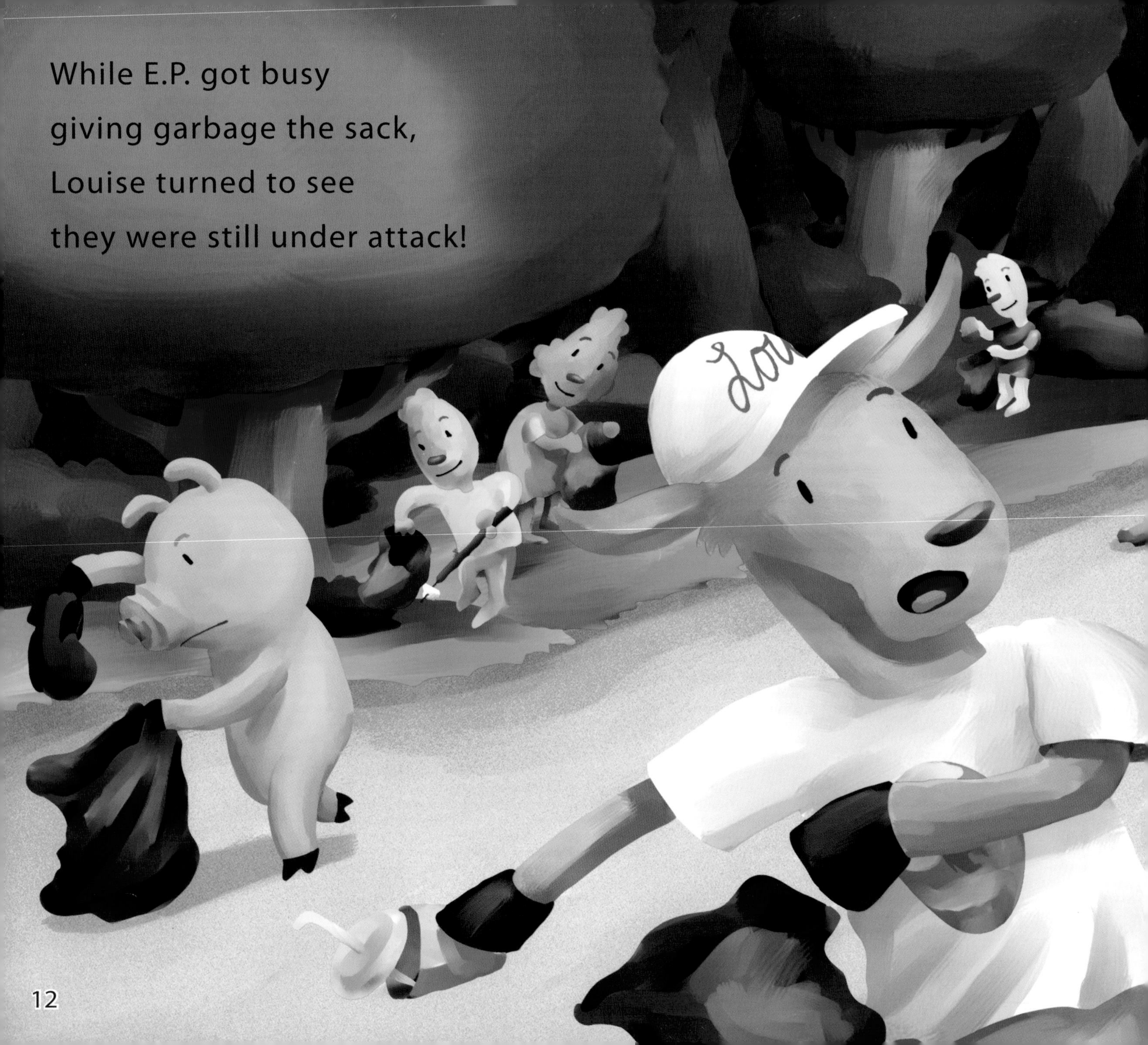

"Hey, how's it going?
I'm Pete J. Pollutes.
How about some chewed bubble gum
or some leaky rain boots?"

“Pardon me, Pete,” said E.P.
“But we keep our town neat,
from the leaves on the trees
to the toes on our feet!”

"Why should I care?" Pete replied.
"I'm just passing through."
"Because all of Earth is your home,"
E.P. said. "It's the right thing to do!

"Just look at this planet!
What a great work of art!
To protect all this beauty,
we must each do our part!

"We all want clean land.
We all want clean water,
every boy, every girl,
every pig, goat, and otter!"

Olive Otter agreed, “When I snorkel and
swim in the peaceful blue sea,
your goop, gunk, and garbage
choke the life out of me!”

"And when I hike in the mountains," added
Louise, "I like to eat what I see.
But I shouldn't eat tin cans,
I'm sure you'll agree."

"That's a whole lot of hogwash," argued Pete.
"You're just a goat and a pig.
You can't make a difference.
The problem's already too big!"

"We can all make a difference," E.P. said.
"We can and we do!
Now kindly put down that litter,
and please join my Green crew!

"Help us clean up this mess,
and let's get on our way.
There are bottles to sort.
It's recycling day!"

Pete finally caught on.

“If you all work to keep our home clean,

then I guess my polluting

is selfish and mean!”

Wiping tears from his eyes,
Pete tossed the boots in the sack.
Then he led that Green crew
as they cleaned their way back.

They cleaned at the beach,

down the mountain, in the park,

and all around the school.

They even cleaned an aardvark!

They recycled paper and cardboard,
plastic bottles and bags,
and tin cans and tinfoil.
They threw out a bunch of greasy old rags.

With each sack that he filled
Pete's smile grew.
He'd made a wonderful discovery—
Earth's beautiful view!

"If you just look around," said E.P.,
"it's easy to care
for the wonder of nature,
for this planet we share."

With a smile and a nod,
Pete linked arms with E.P.
as they watched the sun set
over the green apple tree.

Words to Know

ecology—a branch of science that studies the connection between plants and animals and their environment.

Green—related to or being protective of the environment.

pollute—to make the environment unclean with man-made waste.

recycle—to break down waste, glass, or cans so they can be used again.

Green Facts

- Roadways, forests, parks, and beaches often contain litter. Litter includes: food cartons, Styrofoam cups, napkins, plastic utensils, bottles and cans, paper and plastic bags, clothes, newspapers, magazines, motor oil containers, grease, tires, and much more.

- It can take 1 million years for a glass bottle to decompose, or break down into nothing. Plastic or foam cups and aluminum cans take up to 500 years to decompose.

- Each year, Americans throw out enough plastic bottles to circle the earth four times.

- One pound of newspaper can be recycled to make six cereal boxes, six egg cartons, or 2,000 sheets of writing paper!

- Recycling one aluminum can saves enough energy to light a 100-watt bulb for 3.5 hours.

More Ways to Green-i-fy!

Talk to your mom and dad about what you can try at home:

1. Reduce the amount of garbage that you create.
2. Take your trash with you. Don't leave it behind.
3. Pick up trash that others have left behind.
4. Pre-cycle: Only buy things that come in packages that can be recycled.
5. Recycle plastic, paper, and newspaper.
6. Recycle glass bottles and aluminum cans.
7. Instead of throwing away toys, books, or clothing, donate them to a hospital, a library, or the Salvation Army.